UNDER BMX

BY JAKE MADDOX

Text by Andom Ghebreghiorgis
Illustrated by Sean Tiffany

STONE ARCH BOOKS
a capstone imprint

Jake Maddox Sports Stories is published by
Stone Arch Books
A Capstone Imprint
1710 Roe Crest Drive
North Mankato, Minnesota 56003
www.capstonepub.com

Text and illustrations © 2020 Stone Arch Books

All rights reserved. No part of this publication may be reproduced in whole
or in part, or stored in a retrieval system, or transmitted in any form or by any
means, electronic, mechanical, photocopying, recording, or otherwise, without
written permission of the publisher.

Library of Congress Cataloging-in-Publication Data
Names: Maddox, Jake, author. | Ghebreghiorgis, Andom, author. | Tiffany,
    Sean, illustrator. | Maddox, Jake. Impact books. Jake Maddox sports story.
Title: Undercover BMX / by Jake Maddox ; written by Andom Ghebreghiorgis;
    illustrated by Sean Tiffany.
Description: North Mankato, Minnesota : Stone Arch Books, a Capstone
    imprint, [2019] | Series: Jake Maddox sports stories | Summary: Basketball
    has always come easily to twelve-year-old Devon Rosario of the Bronx, but
    it's been a long time since he actually enjoyed playing. Devon's father sees
    Devon as the family's second chance at basketball glory, and the pressure of
    that expectation is ruining the game. When Devon sees Jamal, a Yemeni
    refugee, doing BMX tricks on his bike, he sees a way to put fun back into
    sports—provided he can keep his new passion secret from his father.
Identifiers: LCCN 2019006173 | ISBN 9781496583307 (hardcover) | ISBN
    9781496584533 (pbk.) | ISBN 9781496583321 (ebook pdf)
Subjects: LCSH: BMX freestyle (Stunt cycling)—Juvenile fiction. | Basketball
    stories. | Puerto Ricans—New York (State)—New York—Juvenile fiction. |
    Fathers and sons—Juvenile fiction. | Secrecy—Juvenile fiction. | Refugees—
    Juvenile fiction. | Friendship—Juvenile fiction. | Bronx (New York, N.Y.)—
    Juvenile fiction. | CYAC: BMX freestyle (Stunt cycling)—Fiction. |
    Basketball—Fiction. | Puerto Ricans—New York (State)—New York—
    Fiction. | Fathers and sons—Fiction. | Secrets—Fiction. | Refugees—
    Fiction. | Friendship—Fiction. | Bronx (New York, N.Y.)—Fiction.
Classification: LCC PZ7.M25643 Un 2019 | DDC 813.6 [Fic]—dc23
LC record available at https://lccn.loc.gov/2019006173

Designer: Tracy McCabe

Printed and bound in the USA
PA70

TABLE OF CONTENTS

CHAPTER 1

UNDER PRESSURE

Basketball in the Bronx wasn't easy. Every few blocks there was a court, and everyone thought they had game. But basketball took more than that. It took practice and mental toughness.

Twelve-year-old Devon Rosario and his team, the North Bronx Knights, had those qualities. It was part of what had made them the top youth team in the league for three years running.

On this Friday night, the packed school gym was quieter than it had ever been for a game. Everyone seemed to be holding their breath.

The Knights were down by one point with seventeen seconds left on the clock. They were undefeated this season and on their home court. Losing wasn't supposed to happen.

Devon felt the eyes of the crowd on him. He knew the ball was coming to him. He was going to be the one to win or lose this game— whether he liked it or not.

Leaving the huddle, the Knights stepped onto the court. The other team, the Dyckman Hoopers, was already on the defense. Their players were smacking the court and clapping, trying to intimidate the Knights.

The referee gave the ball to Curtis, the Knights' point guard. Curtis tossed the ball inbounds. At the top of the key, Devon caught it.

Devon held the ball for the final shot. His defender was off him, so he knew he could easily hit a three-pointer. Everything in basketball seemed to come easy to him.

Except having fun, that is, Devon said to himself. He dribbled the ball once with his left hand.

But it didn't really matter if basketball was fun or not anymore. His team was counting on him.

With two seconds left on the clock, Devon jumped into his shooting motion. At the top of his leap, he released the ball. The ball soared through the air. The arc was as perfect as Devon's shooting form.

In a flash, the ball swished through the basket. Three points. A split second later, the buzzer sounded.

Devon's teammates swarmed him. "You did it, Devon! We won! Yeahhhhh!" they screamed.

Everyone jumped up and down in a tight circle. "Ayyyyyyy," they chanted in typical Uptown fashion.

Devon gave a small smile. He should have been happy. The rest of his team was. But if he was being honest, it had been a long time since he'd felt happy playing basketball.

Lately the pressure of being the star player weighed on him. Not to mention the demanding schedule. Practice, games, and weekend tournaments took up every minute of his free time.

It hadn't been like that when he'd first started playing. Back then, Devon and his friends had watched And1 mixtape videos. They'd tried to do the coolest streetball tricks in the park. Basketball had been the ultimate freedom.

But that was then. Now, basketball just wasn't fun anymore.

But a game-winner is always nice, Devon thought, bringing his mind back to the present.

A moment later, Ms. Walker, the team coach, joined them on the court. "Great job, team!" she said. "Devon, amazing shot! We can always count on you."

Devon gave another tight smile. *Yeah, no pressure there,* he thought.

"OK, it's almost eight o'clock, so let's clear the court," the coach said. "Pack up your stuff, and I'll see you all tomorrow at practice."

Ms. Walker patted Devon on his elbow. The team walked to the bench to collect their stuff.

Everyone was pumped, cheering and shouting. Everyone but Devon. He grabbed his belongings and walked across the court to greet his parents.

Devon's mother hurried down from the stands. "My baby! What a great game you played!" she gushed.

"Thanks, Mom," Devon replied. He forced a smile.

Devon's father extended his hand for a silent, congratulatory handshake. But the look on his face made it clear that he had some thoughts on Devon's play.

Devon wasn't sure he wanted to hear them. It seemed like it was always something with his dad. Most of the time it seemed like he was more invested in basketball than Devon was.

Devon held his hand back. Finally Dad said, "You are not going to shake my hand after a game-winning shot?"

Devon quickly held out his hand. "Sorry, Dad," he said.

"That's better," Dad said, gripping Devon's hand firmly. He paused, then released his grip. A moment later, he started pacing back and forth.

Devon waited for the critique he knew was coming.

"I do have one question, though," Dad continued. "Why in the world would you shoot a three-pointer when you're only down by one point?"

Because I had the open shot! Because it went in! Because I've been playing this stupid game long enough to know what I can do and what will work. Leave me alone! You're never satisfied, no matter what. I don't even care anymore.

That's what Devon wanted to say. It's what he played out in his mind. But he couldn't say that to his father. There was just no way. Instead he stayed quiet and hung his head. Basketball might not be fun anymore, but it was his life.

CHAPTER 2

THE KING

Devon went to sleep angry that night. Heading to practice the next day, he still felt anger running through his veins. Nothing he did—even a game-winning shot—was good enough for his father.

It doesn't matter how hard I work or how much effort I put in. Dad will never be satisfied, Devon thought.

He walked out of practice, trailing after his teammates. Truthfully, he'd wanted to skip practice—maybe even quit basketball altogether. But he knew his father would never allow it.

I should have started playing a sport Dad didn't know anything about from the beginning, Devon thought. *Flag football, swimming, martial arts . . .*

Devon's father saw him as the family's second chance at basketball glory. Dad had been a basketball star when he was younger. Unfortunately, he'd injured his knee in high school and had never been able to play in college. Because of that, he seemed intent on making sure Devon was good enough to get a scholarship. That required endless practice.

"You see that fadeaway I hit in the three-on-three last night?" Curtis asked. "You should pay me to teach you my moves!"

"Yeah, yeah!" Julio, the team's lanky small forward, responded. "But you were hitting all your shots, brother! If you keep that up, and Devon keeps scoring forty every night, we can't lose!"

Curtis fist-bumped Julio. "Facts!" he said.

The boys looked to Devon in agreement, but Devon's attention was elsewhere. Across the parking lot outside the gym, he'd spotted a shadowy figure jumping and flipping down the ramps.

Devon couldn't look away. "What is that kid doing?" he wondered aloud.

He walked closer, drawn to the movements. He could just make out a boy on a shiny silver bike. The bike seemed lightweight, but the thick black wheels looked heavy as they skidded along the stair rails. Black pegs attached to the front of the frame.

The boy kept going. Devon was in awe of the gymnastics being done midair. The front of the bike was spinning as the rider glided. The bar seemed detached from the rest of the bike. It seemed dangerous, but the boy was in such control.

"Hey, man, what are you doing?" Devon called.

The boy on the bike ignored him. Curtis and Julio, who'd followed Devon, looked at their friend in shock.

"Devon, what are you doing?" Curtis muttered. "That kid isn't from around here. Nobody talks to him."

"Yeah, man," Julio added. "Quit messing around. Let's get going. We have to get to practice."

Devon nodded. He knew his teammates were right. Coach didn't accept tardiness. Still, he couldn't help glancing back over his shoulder.

In the parking lot, the boy and his bike were soaring through the air. He looked as free as a butterfly. As Devon watched, the boy sped down a wheelchair ramp and used his strength to lift the bike in the air.

When he landed, he balanced on the bike's front wheel. The back of the bike rose in the air like a seesaw.

Devon's breath caught. He'd seen people riding bikes to get from place to place, but he'd never seen someone do what this boy was doing. Standing upright on his bike, he looked like a king.

CHAPTER 3

REBELLION

The next afternoon, Devon opened his phone to the sound of a calendar chime. *REPORT TO BASKETBALL PRACTICE!* the automatic alert read.

Devon sighed. *It's not enough for Dad to be all over me at games?* he thought. *Now he's invaded my phone too?*

Devon quickly scrolled through the rest of his weekly calendar. He had a social studies test on West African religions in two days, but he was barely going to have time to study. He had practice today, another practice tomorrow, and a note for Saturday that just said, *Meeting with Dad.*

Devon felt overwhelmed. He'd loved basketball once. He was good at it, and he enjoyed the competition. But too often, it took over his life. He missed the freedom of playing for fun.

Speaking of freedom . . . , Devon thought. He thought of the boy he'd seen outside the gym yesterday. He'd ridden his bike with the kind of freedom Devon hadn't felt in forever.

Feeling inspired, Devon grabbed his own bike out of the garage. The tires were a little flat, but it would do. He decided to bike to practice. He had plenty of time. Maybe he'd get lucky and see that boy outside the gym again.

Sure enough, the boy was in the parking lot when Devon arrived. The other boy popped a wheelie and gave Devon a nod. Then he circled around and rode to the handrail next to the gym.

As Devon watched, the boy jumped his bike into the air. He caught the left pegs on the rail—*clink!*—and the bike stopped in the air for a second.

The boy looked toward Devon and pushed his pegs off the rail. He did a three-hundred-and-sixty-degree spin before landing back on the ground. Finally, he turned to Devon.

"So you came to see more?" the boy asked.

Devon couldn't help noticing his heavy Middle Eastern accent. "Do you go to our school? Where'd you learn how to do that?" he asked. "I'm Devon, by the way."

"Yeah, man, I've seen you around," the boy said. "I'm Jamal."

"Where'd you learn to do that?" Devon repeated.

Jamal gave Devon an up-and-down look. He seemed to be deciding whether he could trust him or not.

"Yemen," he finally said. "We had a war, so my brother and I came here. But back home, my uncle gave me a bike. Because of the bombs, there were always obstacles. I learned how to make tricks of them."

"Dang, man. That's something. I'm sorry. My family is from Trinidad and Puerto Rico. In this neighborhood almost everyone's family comes from the Caribbean. They have some violence there too, I know."

"Not just violence," Jamal said. "War."

"Yeah, my bad," Devon said. "You're amazing, though! I'd love to learn to ride like you."

"Takes a lot of practice," Jamal said. "I've been here almost a year now. Got me a good bike now, and I ride in different areas. I'm taking over this parking lot now."

"Definitely. Do your thing! I'm just going to take notes," Devon said with a smile.

Jamal pushed his shoes hard into the bike's pedals and took off. He pedaled toward the end of the parking lot. Just as it looked like he was about to crash, he bunny-hopped, using his strength to turn the bike midair. Then he rode off at a right angle.

Devon was amazed by how strong Jamal seemed to be. The other boy lifted the front wheel high into the air and leaned back as if he was reclining in a chair. He continued riding with no fear of falling. Devon had seen kids in the neighborhood pop a wheelie before, but he'd never seen someone do it for so long.

After Jamal had wheelied around the perimeter of the parking lot, he transitioned into a new trick. He bounced up and down on his back wheel effortlessly. It was almost as if he was using the bike like a pogo stick.

It almost looks like a basketball drill, Devon thought.

But it was so much better than any drill. Jamal was like a ballerina, a figure skater, a break-dancer. He combined death-defying tricks with flashy poses like a true Bronx kid. He rode with ease and flair. He looked as free as Devon used to feel back when he used to play streetball.

Devon couldn't take his eyes off the scene in front of him. All he could think was, *I have to get on that bike.*

CHAPTER 4

PRACTICE

All week long, Devon got to the gym early so he could watch Jamal ride before practice. The two boys had exchanged cell phone numbers after their first meeting. That way they'd be able to meet up.

Devon made sure to stay out of sight in the rear parking lot at the gym. He couldn't risk anyone seeing him. He hadn't told his teammates or parents about his new interest in BMX. He'd considered talking to his mom, but he was fairly certain she'd tell Dad.

Dad would never understand me wanting to try something new, Devon thought. *Basketball is his life.*

But on Thursday, Devon was cutting it a little close. He looked at the time on his phone as he biked up to the gym. Practice would be starting in ten minutes.

I have time, Devon thought to himself. *Maybe Jamal will let me do a quick ride of my own today.*

Devon approached the parking lot and spotted Jamal pedaling quickly. Jamal went down the ramp, shot into the air, and tried to kick his legs off the back pedals. He sort of looked like a frog out of water.

Devon biked over to where Jamal stood with his own bike. He dismounted and looked at his new friend.

"Hey, man. What's up?" he asked. "What was that?"

Jamal gave him a nod. "Hey," he replied. "That's the Superman. Or it's supposed to be. I'll get it . . . eventually. Heading to practice?"

"Yeah, in a few minutes," Devon said. "I've been wanting to ask, though . . . can I try out your bike?"

Jamal stopped and looked at Devon. "This bike is all I've got, man," he said. "Don't play games with me."

"I'm not playing," Devon assured him. "I've been watching you ride all week. Come on, man. I'm ready to ride. I'll be careful with it."

With a last look, Jamal got off his bike and handed it to Devon. He passed him his helmet as well.

Devon shook his head at the offer. "Nah, I don't need that," he said. "I'm good, man."

"No, you're not," Jamal said. "Real ballers stretch, even if you hate it. And real riders wear helmets."

Devon disagreed, but it didn't seem like Jamal was going to budge. Reluctantly he strapped on the helmet. Then he hopped on the bike. Devon was as tall as Jamal, although not as muscular, so the bike was the right height.

"Use your whole body to control the bike," Jamal instructed. "It's not just about using your arms. And start off easy. Remember, if the bike falls, you fall. So don't let the bike fall."

Devon nodded, then started pedaling. The fall air felt cool on his face. He rode around the parking lot, trying to pick up speed.

Across the lot, Jamal yelled, "It's not about speed! It's about control."

Devon ignored his friend. He passed Jamal and looped around the back of the parking lot. He headed straight toward the handrail.

Just like with the game-winning shot, Devon had a decision to make.

Should I try to hop the curb and drift the back wheel? he thought.

He was eager to learn Jamal's peg trick on the handrail. But he was new to BMX and figured that trick was way out of his league.

Fancy slide it is, Devon decided, focusing his gaze straight ahead.

Jamal yelled out, "Slow down, bro! You're going too fast!"

But Devon charged ahead. He was no longer pedaling but gliding through the parking lot. He stood up tall, ready to lift the bike up right before the curb.

As the curb approached, Devon bent his knees to get enough strength to lift the bike. He pulled up with his biceps, and the bike lifted. It was a lot heavier than he'd imagined.

Wow! Jamal is really strong, Devon realized.

Devon was ready for his moment. He imagined it in his mind. Right before landing in front of the handrail, he'd hold the front brake and turn the wheels sharply to the right. The bike's front wheel would stay fixed, but the back wheel would slide in a semicircle. Devon would smoothly turn back to Jamal.

But things didn't go according to plan. As Devon landed, the gym door flew open. Devon's breath caught. Curtis, Julio, the rest of the basketball team, and Ms. Walker stood there. Their mouths opened in shock as they saw Devon heading toward them on the bike.

Devon realized in horror that he'd lost track of time. Practice was over.

The front wheel held as Devon had planned, but the surprise had thrown him off-balance. The bike toppled over. Devon landed with a painful thud on his left elbow. He looked up to see Curtis and Julio standing over him, looking shocked.

CHAPTER 5

GROUNDED

School. Basketball. Staring at the wall. Those were the only things Devon had to focus on during his grounding. Two weeks for semi-accidentally missing one practice.

Devon found it harsh. He'd tried to explain to his parents that it had been an accident. But his teammates had been irritated, and Dad hadn't wanted to hear it.

As far as Dad was concerned, there was no excuse for blowing off basketball. The two-week punishment was his way of forcing Devon to focus.

But it wasn't working. In fact, it was having the opposite effect. The more Devon's father pushed him toward basketball, the less Devon wanted to play it.

What Devon *actually* wanted to do was ride.

Not that anyone seems to care, Devon thought miserably.

The time he'd spent on Jamal's bike had made him feel free. He wanted to be as good at BMX as he was at basketball. It was a new personal challenge.

When he wasn't at school or attending mandatory basketball practices, Devon soaked up online videos of BMX tricks. His favorite was BMX street. Those athletes turned the bike park into their own personal playgrounds.

BMX vert was a close second. Devon loved seeing how much air the riders could get off the ramps. It reminded him of dunking a basketball.

Because they were in different classes at school, Devon hadn't seen Jamal in almost two weeks. He certainly hadn't been able to try any more BMX tricks.

After Coach Walker called his parents, Devon's dad had taken to texting her to make sure Devon got to practice on time. And after practice, Dad was right there, waiting to pick Devon up.

But even the grounding couldn't put a damper on Devon's interest in BMX. He couldn't stop thinking about Jamal attempting the Superman.

Devon must have watched more than a hundred videos of people doing the trick. In all the videos, the riders removed both feet from the pedals and kicked them outward to resemble Superman mid-flight. It was a tough move that required a lot of core strength.

Sometimes riders would extend their legs out with too much force and struggle to time the landing. In other videos, it looked like riders didn't have the ab strength to get their legs high enough.

Devon knew the move was probably too hard for a beginner. But he still couldn't help imagining himself doing it. He was determined to get back on a bike, whether his parents liked it or not.

* * *

The day before Devon's grounding was due to end, Mom knocked on his door. "Can we talk?" she asked, opening the door a crack.

Devon shrugged and continued to sulk. Mom must have taken it as a yes, because she came into the room. Devon avoided her gaze and instead stared up at the posters of famous Knicks players on the walls. He wasn't in the mood for another lecture.

"I wanted to talk to you about basketball," Mom said. "You made a commitment to your team, and skipping practice breaks that promise. Is this going to happen again?"

"That's not really up to me, is it?" Devon snapped.

Mom fixed Devon with a no-nonsense gaze. "It's entirely up to you," she said. "If you go to practice when you're supposed to go to practice, we won't have any more problems."

Devon sighed, feeling frustrated. "Sorry, Mom," he apologized. "It's just . . . I used to love basketball. It used to be fun. But now it feels like it takes up everything. There's no time for anything else. And it's all Dad cares about."

Devon's mother paused to think. "And this change in attitude is due to what? Bike riding?" she asked. "You clearly like it enough to miss basketball practice."

"BMX freestyle," Devon responded eagerly. "I'm obsessed. It's not as easy as basketball. But when I did it, it was just about me, you know? And it was fun."

"I have no idea what BMX is," Mom admitted.

"Let me show you a video," Devon said. He loaded one of the Superman videos he'd been watching on repeat.

Mom watched, looking interested but concerned. When the trick was finished, she said, "Look, Devon, I want you to be happy. Your father and I both do. We want you to challenge yourself and to try new things."

"Sure doesn't feel like it," Devon muttered under his breath.

"You have to be open with us," Mom told him. "You can't go behind our backs when you have a schedule."

"Even if that schedule isn't fair?" Devon argued.

"If there's something you want changed, come to me and your father," Mom said. "Tell us why. Give us reasons with respect. Talk to your dad. Convince him."

Devon looked back at the YouTube video and sighed. He was pretty sure he would have to *be* Superman to convince his father to let him do anything other than basketball.

CHAPTER 6

TUCK NO HANDER

The day after his grounding ended, all Devon could think about was meeting up with Jamal. After two weeks of nothing but online videos, he was desperate for another chance on the bike. When Devon arrived at the gym, Jamal was waiting.

"Hey, man," Jamal greeted him. Devon hopped off his street bike. "Long time no see."

"Long time no ride," Devon replied. "I've been going crazy cooped up at home. Any chance I can get back on your bike? I've been watching videos of the Tuck No Hander online. I really want to give it a try."

"Watching it online isn't the same thing as riding in real life," Jamal said. "That's a risky move. You need to build up to it."

"We learned about Frederick Douglass in history class this year when we talked about the Civil War. Without struggle, there is no progress, my guy! Go big or go home," Devon said proudly.

Jamal shot Devon some serious side-eye. "Yeah, and without practice there are broken bones," he said in retort. But still, he gave Devon his bike.

Devon rolled the bike to the other end of the parking lot and walked it up to the top of the ramp. The L-shaped ramp didn't have barriers, so he'd be able to jump for the solid air needed for the trick. Once he was there, he'd need to tuck his knees under the handlebars and raise his hands in the air.

Devon got ready. He sat on the bike and pedaled down the ramp. As he reached the bottom, he lifted the bike up with impressive strength. He tucked his knees under the handlebars. As he soared through the air, he released his hands from the handlebars.

Almost immediately, he felt himself lose control. Devon quickly brought his knees back to the original position and placed his hands back on the bars.

The bike smacked down on the ground. Devon managed to get his right leg on the ground just in time to stop himself from taking a spill.

"Whoa, that was intense!" Devon yelled.

"You had it for like point-one seconds, brotha!" Jamal exclaimed. "You'll get better with more practice. You just need to get comfortable having your hands off the bike. Try doing it with only one hand this time."

Devon went up the stairs again to try one more time. This time, however, his beginner's luck had run out.

When Devon tried to remove his left hand from the handlebars, he lost his balance. He almost fell over backward, but he curled his body forward to grab the handlebar.

He landed standing upright, but the bike bounced off the ground—hard. The impact vibrated through Devon's body.

"OK, I think that's enough riding for today," Jamal said. "You'll get it next time. It's a pretty complicated move. But I like to think 'complicated' just means you haven't practiced enough to make it easy."

Devon said nothing in reply. He couldn't remember the last time he'd tried something in basketball and been unsuccessful. More than anything, he wanted the freedom Jamal had on the bike.

But he repeated Jamal's words in his head. *Complicated just means you haven't practiced enough.* And Devon wanted to practice. He wanted to stay on the bike as long as he could.

CHAPTER 7

GAME TIME

For fans of the North Bronx Knights, it was easy to see that Devon was not his usual self on the court during Friday night's game. He had been out of sync with his team all week. And now his back was sore from his failed attempt at the Tuck No Hander.

The Knights beat the Liberators 80–47, but Devon had six turnovers. His defense was slow, and his heart wasn't in the game.

After the game, his teammates celebrated their victory. Devon made a beeline toward his parents.

Dad's disappointment was clear on his face. Outside, he finally broke the silence.

"You know, son, the next game is . . . ," Dad began.

But Devon was not paying attention to his father's words. On the other side of the parking lot, Jamal was at the top of the ramp.

Devon's parents followed his gaze. His mother could clearly see her son's fascination. He was hooked.

But Dad was less thrilled. "Who is that boy?" he asked. "Is he the one you were biking with before? The boy who got you into that mess with practice?"

Devon didn't answer any of his father's questions. His eyes were fixed on Jamal. The other boy flew down the ramp and into the air above the parking lot. Jamal kept pedaling midair.

Devon recognized the trick from the videos he'd seen online. It was called ET, just like the movie.

Devon's father looked livid. "Where is this school's security? Or your coach?" he demanded.

Devon couldn't hold his tongue any longer. "Stop, Dad! That's my friend, Jamal. He's the one who introduced me to BMX. He's cool, and I love it, and it's just— "

"Enough!" Dad interrupted. "You're a basketball player. End of story. I'm not going to watch you throw away all our hard work on some new hobby. Get in the car now."

CHAPTER 8

COMPROMISE

The next afternoon, Devon was in his room. There was no practice today, but both his parents were home. Sneaking out to meet Jamal wasn't going to happen.

Devon had retreated to his room with the excuse of doing homework. Truthfully, though, he was mostly watching freestyle BMX online again.

Suddenly Mom yelled from the living room: "Devon, come down here, please!"

Devon sighed. He pressed pause on the video he'd been watching of a BMX rider landing the Tuck No Hander.

In the living room, he found his parents sitting on the sofa waiting for him. They looked serious.

Devon stopped in his tracks when he saw their expressions. "Is everything OK?" he asked.

"Why don't you take a seat, Devon?" his mother replied.

Devon scanned the room anxiously. *Great. What did I manage to do wrong now?* he wondered.

Devon's father spoke first. "Your mother brought something to my attention after last night's game," he began. "Apparently I haven't been very patient—or a good listener. I apologize for that. If there's something you'd like to discuss with me, I'm ready to listen."

Devon couldn't believe how calm his father sounded. *This is my chance,* he thought. *I have to make him see my side.*

Devon took a deep breath. "Here's the thing," he said. "I know you love basketball. I do too. And I know I made a commitment to the team."

Devon paused, and Mom gave him a reassuring nod. "Go on," she said.

"But it's just a lot," Devon continued. "To be honest, it's not fun anymore, and it takes up *all* my time. We have practice almost every day and the game schedule is intense. Plus I have tournaments on the weekend. I have other things I'm interested in and—"

"Like what?" Devon's father interrupted him.

Devon hesitated before continuing. "Well, you know the BMX rider you saw outside the parking lot?" he said. "Like I said, he's actually my friend. I've been learning how to ride from him."

"Your mother tells me you like this . . . a lot. Is that the case?"

"Yes, it is," Devon replied.

"And what do you propose happens to basketball?" Mom asked.

"I don't know," Devon admitted. "I still want to play. Maybe I can take a break from tournaments on the weekend so that I have more free time."

Dad thought for a minute. Then he said, "I hear what you're saying."

"Really?" Devon interrupted.

Dad held up a hand to silence his son. "Look, Devon, you have an immense talent," he continued. "I wouldn't be doing my job as a father if I didn't help you develop your strengths. As good as I was when I was a kid, I wish I'd had the opportunity to go to college. To see where basketball could've taken me."

"I'm not saying I want to give up basketball altogether," Devon argued.

"And I'm not saying I'm against other sports or doing bike tricks," Dad said. "Believe it or not, I get it. We used to do that in San Juan as kids all the time. This is the Bronx, though. You've got cops and lots of cars. I don't want you doing anything that could get you hurt or into trouble."

Devon nodded, too afraid to speak. He didn't want to interrupt his dad when it seemed like they might finally be getting somewhere.

"We can cut back on some tournaments, and you can ride—when it doesn't interfere with basketball," Dad continued. "But let's go to the bike park in the South Bronx. It's safer and more controlled."

Devon jumped out of his chair and gave his father a hug. Dad hugged him back.

Mom smiled at them and left the room. When she returned, she had her hands behind her back.

"Devon, you're definitely your father's son," Mom said. "You're both so stubborn. Both of you just need some communication skills."

She held out her hands.

Devon couldn't believe what he saw. It was a new black helmet. On the back were stickers of the Puerto Rican and Trinidadian flags.

"If you're going to keep riding, you need your own helmet," Mom said. "I watched the videos you showed me. All those riders had helmets on. Plus we figured you could use it with . . ." She paused. "You know what, go check the kitchen."

Devon's parents exchanged a look. In that moment, Devon knew. Whatever was coming, Dad was in on it too.

Devon walked to the kitchen, not sure what—or who—he'd find there.

Ms. Walker? Dirty dishes to clean? The puppy I wanted for my eighth birthday? he thought.

But it was better than anything he could have imagined. Used. Rusty red. Dull pegs. But it was his. Devon's first BMX bike.

CHAPTER 9

HOME COURT

Three months later, sitting on a bench in the South Bronx bike park, Devon's father looked happy and relaxed, if a bit out of place. He was the only person over forty there, but somehow, he belonged. Over the past few months, he had become a sort of coach to Devon and some of the other BMX riders.

At first Devon had been a little worried that Dad's enthusiasm might turn into the same pressure it had with basketball. But they seemed to have reached a compromise. Devon still played basketball, although less frequently than before. In return, Dad supported Devon's BMX riding.

Just then, Jamal got air on the vert.

Dad stood up from the bench and cupped his hands around his mouth. "Get higher, Jamal!" he shouted. "Control your breathing!"

Midair, Jamal grinned.

Curtis and Julio had been coming to the bike park with Devon. Mostly to watch and somtimes to try out a trick on Devon's bike.

For newbies, they weren't bad. Curtis was catching on quickly. Julio was so tall that just standing upright on the bike was impressive.

And then there was Devon, cutting through obstacles like a slasher getting to the lane. He glanced over at his father and saw Dad mutter something under his breath. Devon knew what he was saying: "Ten seconds."

This was it, the last shot.

Should I try to get some air and do some spins? Devon wondered. *Or do a big trick as the grand finale?*

But he remembered what Jamal had said to him when he'd first started riding. *"Complicated" just means you haven't practiced enough to make it easy.*

It still wasn't easy, but Devon was getting there.

Devon saw a mini-ramp and picked up speed heading toward it. He hit the ramp, and his bike lifted high into the air.

Devon tightened his abs and tucked his knees underneath the handlebars. Then, like a gymnast, he extended his arms and straightened his back.

He had no ball in his hand, but he was flying. Tuck No Hander. No problem.

AUTHOR BIO

Andom Ghebreghiorgis was born in New York, New York, to parents who emigrated from Eritrea. After graduating from Yale University in 2007, he taught middle school special education in the Bronx for three years and in Washington Heights for four years. In his free time, Andom loves playing basketball and flag football, spending time with his family and friends, and reading.

ILLUSTRATOR BIO

Sean Tiffany has worked in the illustration and comic book field for more than twenty years. He has illustrated more than sixty children's books for Capstone and has been an instructor at the famed Joe Kubert School in northern New Jersey. Raised on a small island off the coast of Maine, Sean now resides in Boulder, Colorado, with his wife, Monika, their son, James, a cactus named Jim, and a room full of entirely too many guitars.

GLOSSARY

automatic (aw-tuh-MAT-ik)—happening or done without thought or effort

compromise (KOM-pruh-mahyz)—an agreement reached by each side changing or giving up some demands

critique (kri-TEEK)—a careful judgment in which you give your opinion about the good and bad parts of something

detached (dih-TACHT)—not joined or connected

fascination (fas-uh-NEY-shuhn)—a great interest in or attraction to something

immense (ih-MENS)—very great in size or amount

intimidate (in-TIM-i-deyt)—to frighten, especially by threats

livid (LIV-id)—very angry

mandatory (MAN-duh-tawr-ee)—required by law or by a command

retort (ri-TAWRT)—to reply with an argument against

vert (vurt)—an abbreviation for vertical and a term used in BMX to describe a competition held on a vert ramp, which allows riders to fly into the air and land back on the ramp

DISCUSSION QUESTIONS

1. Devon is convinced his parents, especially his dad, won't understand his interest in BMX. Do you think he was right or wrong to assume that? Talk about some other ways he could have handled the situation.

2. Have you ever felt pressured into continuing an activity you no longer found fun? What was it? Talk about how you resolved the situation.

3. Imagine how Devon's basketball teammates, especially Curtis and Julio, might have felt when they learned about Devon's interest in BMX. Talk about their possible feelings. How would you have reacted if you were in their position?

WRITING PROMPTS

1. Jamal mentions that his uncle first got him into BMX when he lived in Yemen. Pretend you are Jamal and write a letter to your uncle, telling him how the bike he gave you shaped your life. Include details about life in the Bronx and how BMX has helped you.

2. Why do you think Devon's father was so determined to have his son play basketball? Write a list of possible reasons, using specific examples from the story to support your argument.

3. Why do you think basketball is so big in Devon's neighborhood, the Bronx? Make a list of reasons, using facts from the story and outside research to help you.

MORE ABOUT BMX

BMX captures Devon's attention from the moment he sees Jamal on his bike. Are you as intrigued as he was? To learn more, check out these quick facts about BMX.

BMX, which stands for "bicycle motocross," is an extreme sport and form of cycling.

The sport of BMX was first created in Southern California in the 1970s by young riders who were inspired by motocross, an off-road form of motorcycling. It gained popularity in the United States and throughout the world from there.

A BMX bike has several unique features. It is much smaller than a typical road bike and has a strong frame with twenty-inch wheels and high handlebars.

BMX first made its debut as an Olympic sport in 2008 at the Beijing Olympic Games.

BMX can be divided into BMX racing or freestyle BMX. BMX racing involves off-road racing events, in which riders compete to finish a course in the fastest time. In freestyle BMX, riders perform complicated tricks as they move through an urban space, a BMX park, a vert ramp, trails, or flatland.

BMX flatland and street tricks tend to require on-the-ground balance. Freestyle dirt BMX and vert-ramp riding have a lot more aerial tricks than the other disciplines.

Some famous BMX riders, considered legends in the sport, include Mat Hoffman, Dave Mirra, Ryan Nyquist, and Tinker Juarez.

Women's BMX is also gaining traction thanks to talented female riders, including Nina Buitrago and Hannah Roberts.

MORE FROM JAKE MADDOX!

- BLUE LINE BREAKAWAY
- PICK AND ROLL
- DIAMOND DOUBLE PLAY
- UNDERCOVER BMX

FIND MORE AT CAPSTONEPUB.COM

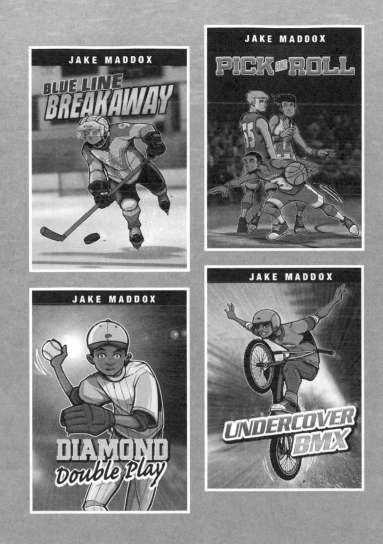

READ THEM ALL !

THE FUN DOESN'T STOP HERE!

DISCOVER MORE AT:
www.capstonekids.com

**AUTHORS AND ILLUSTRATORS
VIDEOS AND CONTESTS
GAMES AND PUZZLES
HEROES AND VILLAINS**